THIS BOOK BELONGS TO

....

My WONDERFUL NURSERY RHYME Collection

BONNEY
PRESS

Published by Bonney Press,
an imprint of Hinkler Books Pty Ltd 2015
45-55 Fairchild Street
Heatherton Victoria 3202 Australia
www.hinkler.com.au

BONNEY
PRESS

© Hinkler Books Pty Ltd 2015

Illustrators: Steph Baxter, Sarah Coleman, Jon Contino, Sarah Dennis, Nicolò Giacomin & Lucia Calfapietra, Lauren Hom, Lalalimola, Mick Marston, Jess Matthews, Chris Robertson, Marie Simpson, Alice Stevenson, Yulia Vysotskaya.

ISBN: 978 1 7436 7754 4

Printed and bound in China

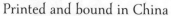

INTRODUCTION

Reading nursery rhymes aloud with children is a joyful experience that helps foster a love for reading and the spoken word.

Nursery Rhymes are found in every culture and have a rich, oral-folktale history that has developed throughout the ages. The simple rhythms, catchy rhymes and colourful characters of nursery rhymes intrinsically appeal to children and are designed to be read-aloud.

Not only do nursery rhymes engage the imagination of even the youngest children, but they inspire engagement with the world around them; for example, through the onomatopoeic nursery rhyme "Old McDonald Had a Farm." They also help children gain an understanding of language, rhythm and rhyme. In fact, the ability of children to recognise and enjoy nursery rhymes has been linked to their progress in reading later on in life.

Nursery-rhyme songs that add simple melody to rhythm, such as "Humpty Dumpty Sat on the Wall" and "Row, Row, Row Your Boat," continue to be a joy to children from generation to generation. Counting nursery rhymes are also a fun and effective way to help develop a child's numeracy skills; for example, in the song "Five Little Monkeys."

Action rhymes, like "This Little Piggy" and "I'm a Little Teapot," involve children acting out the rhymes with their fingers, hands or even their whole body! This adds extra fun to the nursery rhyme experience, emphasises rhythm and can aid a child's understanding of concepts such as numbers and spatial awareness. Similarly, nursery-rhyme games, such as "Ring-a-ring o' Roses" and "Oranges and Lemons," are a fun way to practise coordination, learn concepts and develop social skills. You can find instructions for a range of nursery-rhyme actions on page 66 and nursery-rhyme games on page 128.

Nursery-rhyme lullabies such as "Twinkle, Twinkle, Little Star," are filled with soothing rhymes and rocking rhythms to relax your child or help them to sleep. Lullabies are among the earliest children's songs recorded, and most centre around themes of nurturing and protecting your little one.

So open up worlds of wonder, learning and, most importantly, fun through this stunning collection of nursery-rhyme classics!

CONTENTS

CONTENTS

CONTENTS

HUMPTY DUMPTY sat ON THE WALL

AND OTHER NURSERY RHYME SONGS

Humpty Dumpty sat on the wall,
Humpty Dumpty had a great fall.
All the king's horses and all the king's men
Couldn't put Humpty together again.

Yankee Doodle went to town
Riding on a pony;
He stuck a feather in his hat,
And called it macaroni.

MARY, MARY, QUITE CONTRARY HOW DOES YOUR GARDEN GROW? WITH SILVER BELLS AND COCKLE SHELLS, AND PRETTY MAIDS ALL IN A ROW.

It's raining, it's pouring.
The old man is snoring;
He went to bed and bumped his head,
And couldn't get up in the morning.

SING A SONG OF SIXPENCE,
A POCKET FULL OF RYE;
FOUR AND TWENTY BLACKBIRDS,
BAKED in a PIE.
WHEN THE PIE WAS OPENED,
THE BIRDS BEGAN TO SING;
WASN'T THAT A DAINTY DISH,
TO SET BEFORE THE KING?

THE KING WAS IN HIS COUNTING-HOUSE, COUNTING OUT HIS MONEY; THE QUEEN WAS IN THE PARLOUR, EATING BREAD AND HONEY. THE MAID WAS IN THE GARDEN, HANGING OUT THE CLOTHES, WHEN DOWN CAME A BLACKBIRD, AND PECKED OFF HER NOSE.

There was an old woman
Who lived in a shoe,
She had so many children,
She didn't know what to do;
She gave them some broth
Without any bread;
Then whipped them all soundly
And put them to bed.

Rub-a-dub dub,
Three men in a tub,
And who do you think they be?
The butcher, the baker,
The candlestick-maker.
Turn them out, knaves all three.

Sally, go round the Sun
Sally, go round the Moon
Sally, go round the chimneypots
on a Saturday afternoon

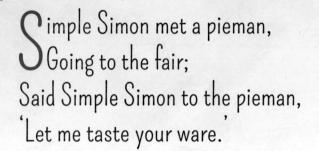

Simple Simon met a pieman,
Going to the fair;
Said Simple Simon to the pieman,
'Let me taste your ware.'

Said the pieman to Simple Simon,
'Show me first your penny';
Said Simple Simon to the pieman,
'Indeed, I have not any.'

Simple Simon went a-fishing,
For to catch a whale;
All the water he had got,
Was in his mother's pail.

Simple Simon went to look
If plums grew on a thistle;
He pricked his fingers very much,
Which made poor Simon whistle.

He went for water in a sieve
But soon it all fell through;
And now poor Simple Simon
Bids you all adieu.

Oh, do you know the muffin man,
The muffin man, the muffin man,
Do you know the muffin man,
Who lives in Drury Lane?

Oh yes, I know the muffin man,
The muffin man, the muffin man,
Yes, I know the muffin man,
Who lives in Drury Lane.

Jack and Jill went up the hill
To fetch a pail of water;
Jack fell down and broke his crown,
And Jill came tumbling after.

Up Jack got and home did trot,
As fast as he could caper;
He went to bed to mend his head
With vinegar and brown paper.

Row, row, row your boat,
Gently down the stream.
Merrily, merrily, merrily, merrily,
Life is but a dream.

Georgie Porgie, pudding and pie,
Kissed the girls and made them cry;
When the boys came out to play,
Georgie Porgie ran away.

Lucy Locket lost her pocket
Kitty Fisher found it
Not a penny was there in it
But a ribbon round it

Polly put the kettle on,
Polly put the kettle on,
Polly put the kettle on,
We'll all have tea.

Sukey take it off again,
Sukey take it off again,
Sukey take it off again,
They've all gone away.

Little Miss Muffet
Sat on a tuffet,
Eating her curds and whey;
Along came a spider,
Who sat down beside her
And frightened Miss Muffet away.

Hot cross buns!
Hot cross buns!
One a penny, two a penny,
Hot cross buns!

If you have no daughters,
Give them to your sons.
One a penny,
Two a penny,
Hot cross buns!

Oh...
the grand old
Duke of York,
He had ten thousand men,
He marched them up
to the top of the hill
And he marched them down again.
And when they were up they were up,
And when they were down they were down;
And when they were only halfway up,
They were neither
up nor down.

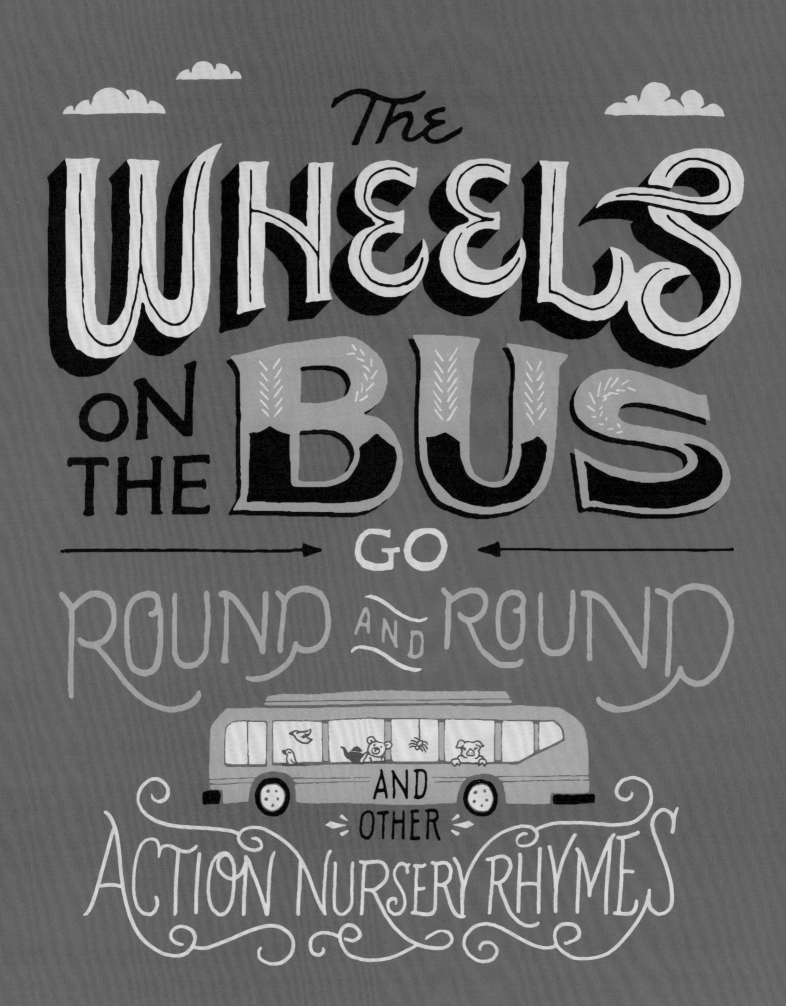

The wheels on the bus go round and round,
Round and round, round and round,
The wheels on the bus go round and round,
All through the town.

The door on the bus goes open and shut...

The wipers on the bus go swish, swish, swish...

The driver on the bus says 'Move on back...'

The people on the bus go up and down...

The babies on the bus go 'Wah, wah, wah...'

The mothers on the bus go 'Shh, shh, shh...'

Round and round the garden,
Like a teddy bear.
One step, two steps,
Tickle you under there!

THIS IS THE WAY THE *Ladies* RIDE,

TRIPPETY-*tee*, TRIPPETY-*tee*!

THIS IS THE WAY THE LADIES RIDE,

Trippety-trippety-tee!

THIS IS THE WAY THE GENTLEMEN RIDE,

JIGGETY-JOG, JIGGETY-JOG!

THIS IS THE *way* THE GENTLEMEN *ride*,

Jiggety-jiggety-jog!

THIS IS THE WAY THE
FARMERS RIDE,
HOBBLEDY-HOY, HOBBLEDY-HOY!
THIS IS THE WAY THE FARMERS RIDE,
HOBBLEDY·HOBBLEDY·HOY!

THIS IS THE WAY
THE HUNTERS RIDE,
GALLOPY-GALLOP, GALLOPY-GALLOP!
THIS IS THE WAY THE hunters RIDE,
GALLOPY-GALLOPY-GALLOP!
AND DOWN INTO THE DITCH!

Incy Wincy Spider
Climbed up the water spout.
Down came the rain
And washed poor Incy out.

Out came the sunshine
And dried up all the rain,
And Incy Wincy Spider
Climbed up the spout again.

Two fat gentlemen met in a lane,
Bowed most politely, bowed once again.
How do you do? How do you do?
How do you do again?

Two thin ladies
met in a lane…

Two tall policemen met in a lane…

Two little schoolboys met in a lane…

Two little babies met in a lane…

END OF ROAD

Five fat sausages frying in a pan
One went POP! And then it went BANG!

Four fat sausages frying in a pan
One went POP! And then it went BANG!

Three fat sausages frying in a pan
One went POP! And then it went BANG!

Two fat sausages frying in a pan
One went **POP**! And then it went **BANG**!

One fat sausage frying in a pan
One went **POP**! And then it went **BANG**!

And there were **NO** sausages left!

This little piggy went to market,
This little piggy stayed home;

This little piggy had roast beef,
This little piggy had none;

And this little piggy cried, 'Wee-wee-wee!'
All the way home.

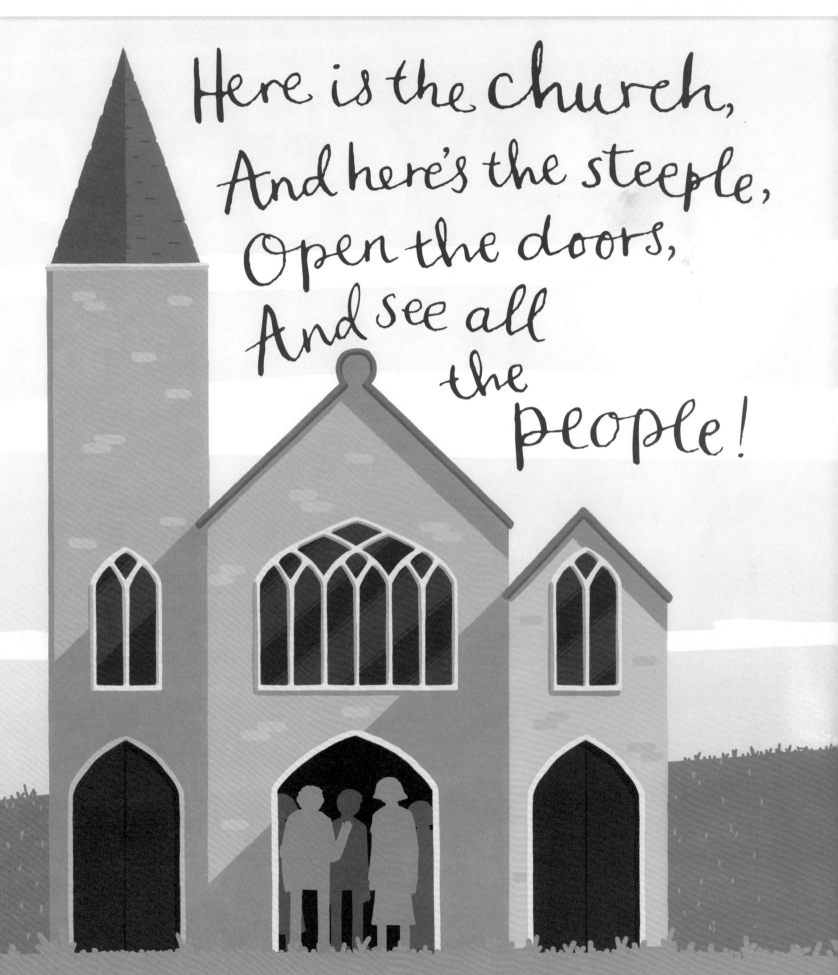

Here is the church,
And here's the steeple,
Open the doors,
And see all the people!

Pat-a-cake, pat-a-cake, baker's man.
Bake me a cake as fast as you can;
Pat it and prick it and mark it with B,
Put it in the oven for baby and me.

WHERE IS THUMBKIN?
WHERE IS THUMBKIN?
HERE I AM! HERE I AM!
How are you today, sir?
VERY WELL,
I THANK YOU.
RUN AWAY. RUN AWAY.

WHERE
IS POINTER? (x2)
HERE I AM! HERE I AM!
HOW ARE YOU TODAY, SIR?
VERY WELL, I THANK YOU.
RUN AWAY. (x2)

Where is Tallman? (x2)
HERE I AM! (x2)
HOW ARE YOU TODAY, SIR?
very well, I thank you.
= RUN AWAY. (x2)

WHERE IS RINGMAN? (x2)
HERE I AM! (x2)
How are you today, sir?
VERY WELL, I THANK YOU.
RUN AWAY. RUN AWAY.

WHERE IS PINKIE? (x2)
HERE I AM! (x2)
HOW ARE YOU TODAY, SIR?
VERY WELL, I THANK YOU.
RUN AWAY. RUN AWAY.

Teddy bear, teddy bear, turn around;
Teddy bear, teddy bear, touch the ground.
Teddy bear, teddy bear, climb the stairs;
Teddy bear, teddy bear, say your prayers.
Teddy bear, teddy bear, turn out the light;
Teddy bear, teddy bear, say good night!

TWO LITTLE DICKY BIRDS,
Sitting on a wall;
ONE NAMED PETER,
ONE NAMED PAUL.

Fly away PETER!
FLY AWAY Paul!
COME BACK PETER!
COME BACK PAUL!

Miss Polly had a dolly who was sick, sick, sick,
So she called for the doctor to come quick, quick, quick.
The doctor came with his bag and his hat,
And he knocked at the door with a rat-a-tat-tat!

He looked at the dolly and he shook his head,
And he said 'Miss Polly, put her straight to bed!'
He wrote on a paper for a pill, pill, pill,
'I'll be back in the morning with my bill, bill, bill.'

I'm a little teapot, short and stout,
Here is my handle, here is my spout.
When I get all steamed up, hear me shout,
Tip me over and pour me out!

I have ten little fingers,
And they all belong to me.
I can make them do things,
Would you like to see?

I can shut them up tight,
Or open them wide.
I can put them together,
Or make them all hide.

I can make them jump high,
I can make them go low.
I can fold them up quietly,
And hold them just so.

Here is the beehive,
But where are the bees?
Hidden away,
Where nobody sees.
Watch and you'll see them
Come out of the hive.
One, two, three, four, five.
Bzzzzzzz!

Action Instructions

The Wheels on the Bus (pages 38-39)

The wheels on the bus go round and round...	(turn hands around each other)
The door on the bus goes open and shut...	(open hands and clap them together)
The wipers on the bus go swish, swish, swish...	(swish arms back and forth like wipers)
The driver on the bus says 'Move on back....'	(point over shoulder with thumb)
The people on the bus go up and down...	(sit up and down)
The babies on the bus go 'Wah, wah, wah...'	(rub eyes as though crying)
The mothers on the bus go 'Shh, shh, shh...'	(put forefinger to mouth)

Round and Round the Garden (pages 40-41)

Round and round the garden, Like a teddy bear.	(circle finger around child's palm)
One step, two steps,	(walk your fingers up child's arm)
Tickle you under there!	(tickle under arm or chin)

This Is the Way the Ladies Ride (pages 42-43)

This is the way the ladies ride...	(place child on knee facing you, bounce gently)
This is the way the gentlemen ride...	(bounce child a little faster but still gently)
This is the way the farmers ride...	(bounce child faster and a little higher)
This is the way the hunters ride...	(bounce child higher and faster)
And down into the ditch!	(lift child up in the air)

Incy Wincy Spider (pages 44-45)

Incy Wincy Spider, Climbed up the water spout.	(alternately touch thumb of one hand to little finger of other)
Down came the rain	(raise hands and wiggle fingers as you lower hands)
And washed poor Incy out.	(sweep hands from side to side)
Out came the sunshine	(raise hands and sweep side to side)
And dried up all the rain,	(raise hands and wiggle fingers)
And Incy Wincy Spider, Climbed up the spout again.	(repeat action for first line)

Two Fat Gentlemen (pages 46-47)

Two fat gentlemen/ladies/policemen/schoolboys/babies met in a lane,	(hold up thumbs/forefinger/middle finger/ring finger/little finger facing each other)
Bowed most politely, bowed once again.	(bow fingers towards each other twice)
How do you do?	(bow one finger towards the other)
How do you do?	(bow the other one finger towards the other)
How do you do again?	(bow fingers towards each other)

Five Fat Sausages (pages 48-49)

Five/Four/Three/Two/One fat sausages frying in a pan,	(hold up five/four/three/two/one fingers and move in a sizzling motion)
One went pop!	(pop cheek with finger)
And then it went BANG!...	(clap hands loudly)
And there were NO sausages left!	(hold up closed fist)

This Little Piggy (pages 50-52)

This little piggy went to market, This little piggy stayed home; This little piggy had roast beef, This little piggy had none;	(touch each of child's toes in turn with each line)
And this little piggy cried, 'Wee-wee-wee!'	(walk fingers up child's leg)
All the way home.	(tickle belly or under arm)

Here Is the Church (page 53)

Here is the church,	(fold hands with fingers crossed inside and thumbs together pointing up)
And here's the steeple,	(raise both forefingers and create a point)
Open the doors,	(open thumbs up)
And see all the people!	(turn hands around and wiggle crossed fingers)

Pat-a-Cake (pages 54-55)

Pat-a-cake, pat-a-cake, baker's man. Bake me a cake as fast as you can;	(clap hands in time with rhyme of rhyme)
Pat it and prick it and mark it with B,	(trace B on palm)
Put it in the oven	(extend both hands)
for baby and me.	(point to baby and self)

Where Is Thumbkin? (pages 56–57)

Where is Thumbkin/Pointer/Tallman/Ringman/Pinkie? (x2)	(place hands behind back)
Here I am!	(bring right hand to front, with thumb/forefinger/middle finger/ring finger/little finger up)
Here I am!	(do the same with the left hand)
How are you today, sir?	(wiggle right thumb or finger)
Very well, I thank you.	(wiggle left thumb or finger)
Run away.	(place right hand behind back)
Run away.	(place left hand behind back)

Teddy Bear, Teddy Bear (pages 58–59)

Teddy bear, teddy bear, turn around;	(turn in circle)
Teddy bear, teddy bear, touch the ground.	(touch floor)
Teddy bear, teddy bear, climb the stairs;	(act climbing stairs)
Teddy bear, teddy bear, say your prayers.	(put hands together like praying)
Teddy bear, teddy bear, turn out the light;	(act blowing out candle)
Teddy bear, teddy bear, say good night!	(rest head on hand and close eyes)

Two Little Dicky Birds (page 60)

Two little dicky birds, Sitting on a wall;	(raise forefinger of each hand)
One named Peter,	(wiggle one finger)
One named Paul.	(wiggle other finger)
Fly away Peter!	(place one hand behind back)
Fly away Paul!	(place other hand behind back)
Come back, Peter!	(bring back one hand with forefinger raised)
Come back, Paul!	(bring back other hand with forefinger raised)

Miss Polly Had a Dolly (page 61)

Miss Polly had a dolly who was sick, sick, sick,	(hold arms as if holding a baby and rock)
So she called for the doctor to come quick, quick, quick.	(place hand to ear like phone and beckon finger)
The doctor came with his bag and his hat,	(raise one hand as if holding a bag, and touch other to head)
And he knocked at the door with a rat-a-tat-tat.	(knocking on door motion)
He looked at the dolly and he shook his head,	(shake head)
And he said 'Miss Polly, put her straight to bed!'	(shake finger as if scolding)
He wrote on a paper for a pill, pill, pill,	(pretend to write on palm with pencil)
'I'll be back in the morning with my bill, bill, bill.'	(hold out paper)

I'm a Little Teapot (pages 62–63)

I'm a little teapot, short and stout,	(stand straight)
Here is my handle,	(put hand on hip for handle)
here is my spout,	(put out bent arm for spout)
When I get all steamed up, hear me shout, Tip me over and pour me out!	(tilt body to the spout side to pour tea)

Ten Little Fingers (page 64)

I have ten little fingers,	(hold up 10 fingers)
And they all belong to me.	(point to self)
I can make them do things, Would you like to see?	(wiggle fingers)
I can shut them up tight,	(make fist)
Or open them wide.	(open hands)
I can put them together,	(place palms together)
Or make them all hide.	(put hands behind back)
I can make them jump high,	(raise hands over head)
I can make them go low.	(touch floor)
I can fold them up quietly, And hold them just so.	(fold hands in lap)

Here Is the Beehive (page 65)

Here is the beehive, But where are the bees? Hidden away, Where nobody sees. Watch and you'll see them, Come out of the hive.	(hold up fist)
One, two, three, four, five.	(count out fingers one at a time)
Bzzzzzzzz	(wiggle fingers)

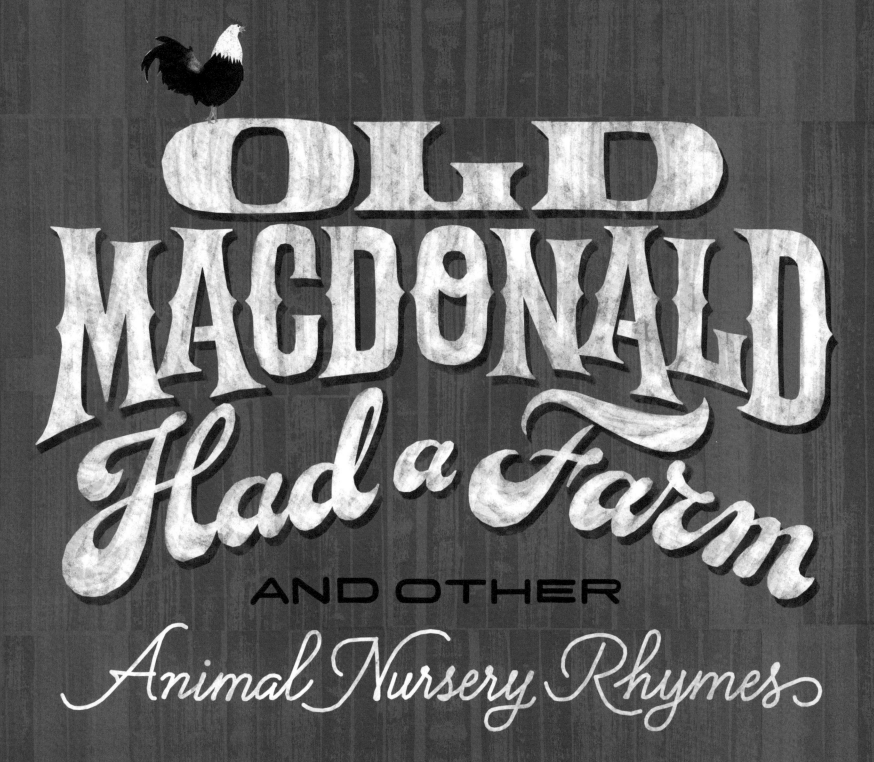

OLD MACDONALD
Had a Farm
AND OTHER
Animal Nursery Rhymes

Old MacDonald had a farm, E-I-E-I-O!
And on that farm he had a cow, E-I-E-I-O!
With a moo moo here and a moo moo there,
Here a moo, there a moo,
Everywhere a moo moo!
Old MacDonald had a farm, E-I-E-I-O!

Old MacDonald had a farm, E-I-E-I-O!
And on that farm he had a pig, E-I-E-I-O!
With an oink oink here and an oink oink there...

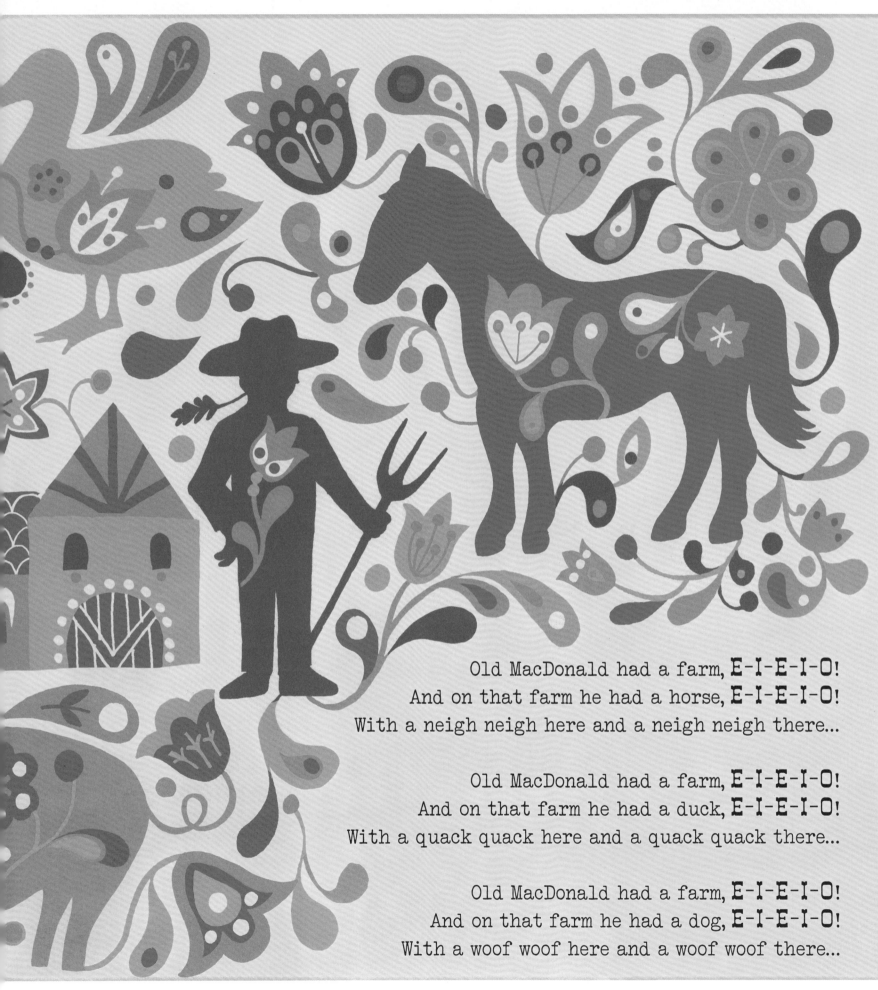

Old MacDonald had a farm, E-I-E-I-O!
And on that farm he had a horse, E-I-E-I-O!
With a neigh neigh here and a neigh neigh there...

Old MacDonald had a farm, E-I-E-I-O!
And on that farm he had a duck, E-I-E-I-O!
With a quack quack here and a quack quack there...

Old MacDonald had a farm, E-I-E-I-O!
And on that farm he had a dog, E-I-E-I-O!
With a woof woof here and a woof woof there...

ONE FOR THE MASTER,
AND ONE FOR THE DAME,
AND ONE FOR THE LITTLE BOY
WHO LIVES DOWN
THE LANE.

Old Mother Hubbard
  Went to the cupboard
To fetch her poor dog a bone;
When she got there,
The cupboard was bare,
And so the poor dog had none.

She went to the baker's
To buy him some bread;
But when she came back,
The poor dog was dead!

She went to the undertaker's
To buy him a coffin;
But when she came back,
The poor dog was laughing.

She went to the fishmonger's
To buy him some fish;
But when she came back,
He was washing the dish.

She went to the hatter's
To buy him a hat;
But when she came back,
He was feeding her cat.

She went to the barber's
To buy him a wig;
But when she came back,
He was dancing a jig.

She went to the fruiterer's
To buy him some fruit;
But when she came back,
He was playing the flute.

She went to the tailor's
To buy him a coat;
But when she came back,
He was riding a goat.

She went to the cobbler's
To buy him some shoes;
But when she came back,
He was reading the news.

She went to the seamstress
To buy him some linen;
But when she came back,
The dog was a-spinning.

She went to the hosier's
To buy him some hose;
But when she came back,
He was dressed in his clothes.

The dame made a curtsy,
The dog made a bow;
The dame said, 'Your servant!'
The dog said, 'Bow-wow!'

Ding, dong, bell,
Pussy's in the well.
Who put her in?
Little JOHNNY GREEN.

Who pulled her OUT?
Little TOMMY STOUT.

What a naughty boy was that,

To try and drown poor pussy cat,

Who never did him any harm,

And killed the mice

in his
father's
barn.

Ride a cock-horse to Banbury Cross,
To see a fine lady upon a white horse;
With rings on her fingers and bells on her toes,
She shall have music wherever she goes.

Hickory, dickory, dock,
The mouse ran up the clock,
The clock struck one,
The mouse ran down,
Hickory, dickory, dock.

Pussycat, pussycat, where have you been?
I've been to London to visit the queen.
Pussycat, pussycat, what did you there?
I frightened a little mouse under her chair.

MARY HAD A LITTLE
LAMB
ITS FLEECE WAS WHITE AS SNOW
AND *everywhere* THAT MARY WENT
THE LAMB WAS *sure* TO GO
IT FOLLOWED HER TO SCHOOL
ONE DAY WHICH WAS AGAINST *the rule*
IT MADE THE CHILDREN
LAUGH AND PLAY
TO SEE A *lamb* AT SCHOOL!

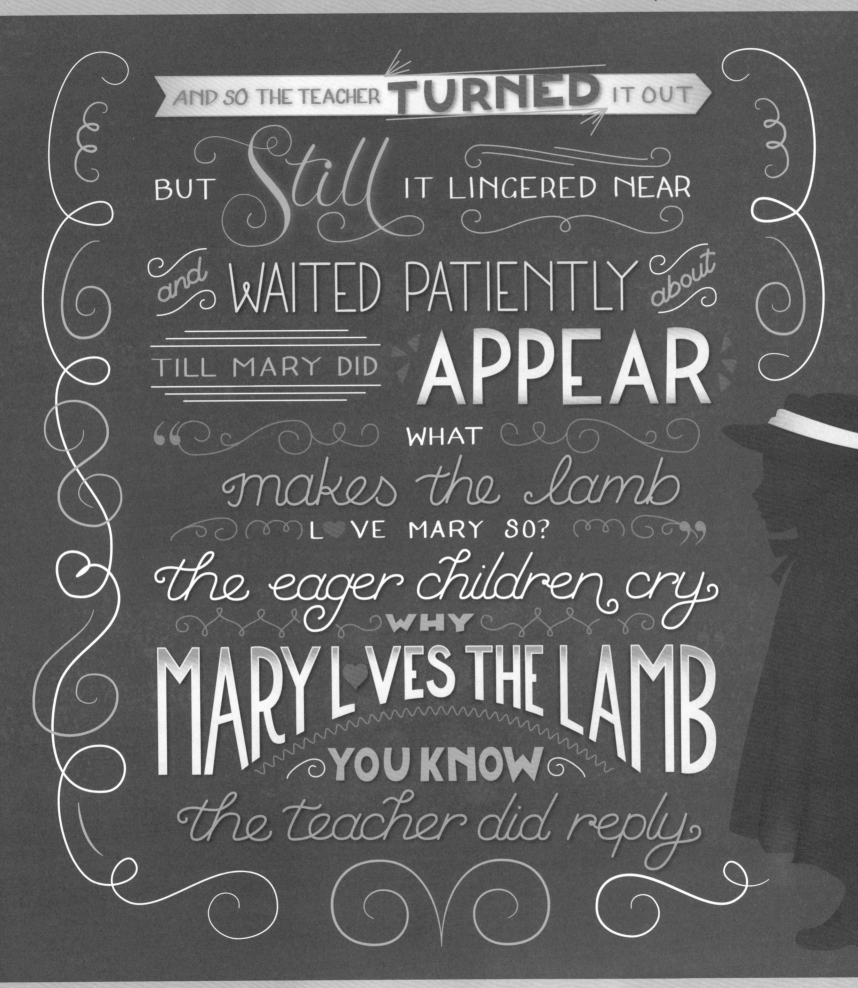

AND SO THE TEACHER TURNED IT OUT

BUT Still IT LINGERED NEAR

and WAITED PATIENTLY about

TILL MARY DID APPEAR

WHAT

makes the lamb

LOVE MARY SO?

the eager children cry

WHY

MARY LOVES THE LAMB

YOU KNOW

the teacher did reply

The Owl and the Pussycat went to sea
In a beautiful pea-green boat;
They took some honey, and plenty of money,
Wrapped up in a five-pound note.
The Owl looked up to the stars above,
And sang to a small guitar,
'O lovely Pussy! O Pussy, my love,
What a beautiful Pussy you are,
You are, you are!
What a beautiful Pussy you are!'

Pussy said to the Owl, 'You elegant fowl!
How charmingly sweet you sing!
O, let us be married; too long we have tarried:
But what shall we do for a ring?'
They sailed away, for a year and a day,
To the land where the bong-tree grows
And there in a wood a Piggy-wig stood,
With a ring at the end of his nose,
His nose, his nose,
With a ring at the end of his nose.

'Dear Pig, are you willing to sell for one shilling
Your ring?' Said the Piggy, 'I will.'
So they took it away, and were married next day
By the turkey who lives on the hill.
They dined on mince and slices of quince,
Which they ate with a runcible spoon;
And hand in hand, on the edge of the sand,
They danced by the light of the moon,
The moon, the moon,
They danced by the light of the moon.

ONCE I SAW A *little bird*

COME HOP hop HOP

So I cried, "LITTLE BIRD

WILL YOU STOP stop STOP ?"

I WAS *going* TO THE *window,*

To say "HOW DO YOU DO ?"

BUT HE *shook* HIS *little* TAIL,

And far away he flew.

Hickety, pickety, my black hen,
She lays eggs for gentlemen;
Gentlemen come every day
To see what my black hen doth lay;
Sometimes nine and sometimes ten,
Hickety, pickety, my black hen.

I love little pussy,
Her coat is so warm,
And if I don't hurt her,
She'll do me no harm.

So I'll not pull her tail,
Nor drive her away,
But pussy and I,
Together will play.

WHAT DO YOU SUPPOSE?
A BEE SAT ON MY NOSE.
THEN WHAT DO YOU THINK?
HE GAVE ME A WINK
AND SAID,
"I BEG YOUR PARDON,
I THOUGHT YOU WERE
THE GARDEN!"

Three little kittens, they lost their mittens,
And they began to cry;
Oh, mother dear, we sadly fear
That we have lost our mittens.
What! Lost your mittens, you naughty kittens!
Then you shall have no pie.
Mee-ow, mee-ow, mee-ow,
No, you shall have no pie.

The three little kittens, they found their mittens,
And they began to cry;
Oh, mother dear, see here, see here,
For we have found our mittens.
Put on your mittens, you silly kittens,
And you shall have some pie.
Purr-r, purr-r, purr-r,
Oh, let us have some pie.

The three little kittens put on their mittens,
And soon ate up the pie;
Oh, mother dear, we greatly fear
That we have soiled our mittens.
What! Soiled your mittens, you naughty kittens!
Then they began to sigh,
Mee-ow, mee-ow, mee-ow,
Then they began to sigh.

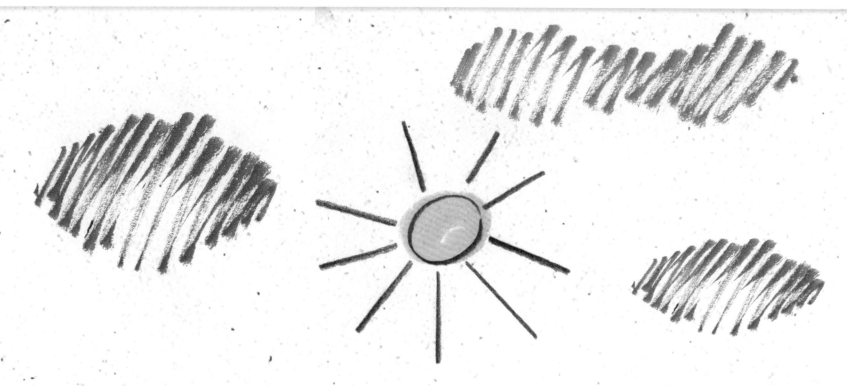

The three little kittens, they washed their mittens,
And hung them out to dry;
Oh, mother dear, do you not hear,
That we have washed our mittens?
What! Washed your mittens, you good little kittens,
But I smell a rat close by.
Mee-ow, mee-ow, mee-ow,
We smell a rat close by.

Higglety
Pigglety
Pop!
The dog has eaten the mop
The pig's in a hurry
The cat's in a flurry
Higglety Pigglety Pop!

Here We Go Round the Mulberry Bush

and Other Nursery Rhyme Games

Here we go round the mulberry bush,
The mulberry bush, the mulberry bush.
Here we go round the mulberry bush,
On a cold and frosty morning.

This is the way we wash our clothes,
Wash our clothes, wash our clothes.
This is the way we wash our clothes,
On a cold and frosty morning.

London Bridge is falling down,
Falling down, falling down.
London Bridge is falling down,
My fair lady.

Build it up with sticks and stones,
Sticks and stones, sticks and stones...

Sticks and stones will wear away,
Wear away, wear away...

Build it up with iron and steel,
Iron and steel, iron and steel...

Iron and steel will bend and bow,
Bend and bow, bend and bow...

Build it up with bricks and clay,
Bricks and clay, bricks and clay...

Bricks and clay will wash away,
Wash away, wash away...

Build it up with silver and gold,
Silver and gold, silver and gold...

Silver and gold will be stole away,
Stole away, stole away...

London Bridge is falling down,
Falling down, falling down...

A-TISKET, A-TASKET, A green AND yellow BASKET. I WROTE a LETTER to MY love, AND on the WAY, I DROPPED IT.

I DROPPED IT, I DROPPED it, AND on THE way, I DROPPED IT. A little BOY PICKED it UP, AND PUT it in HIS POCKET.

Half a pound of tuppenny rice,
Half a pound of treacle.
That's the way the money goes,
Pop goes the weasel!

Every night when I get home
The monkey's on the table.
Take a stick and knock it off,
Pop goes the weasel!

Up and down the City Road
In and out the Eagle.
That's the way the money goes,
Pop goes the weasel!

All around the mulberry bush
The monkey chased the weasel.
The monkey stopped to pull up his sock,
Pop goes the weasel!

The farmer in the dell,
The farmer in the dell,
Hey-ho, the derry-o,
The farmer in the dell.

The farmer takes a wife...

The wife takes the child...

The child takes the nurse...

The nurse takes the cow...

The cat takes the mouse...

The mouse takes the cheese...

The cheese stands alone...

Ring-a-ring o' roses,
A pocket full of posies,
A-TisHoo! A-TisHoo!
We all fall down.

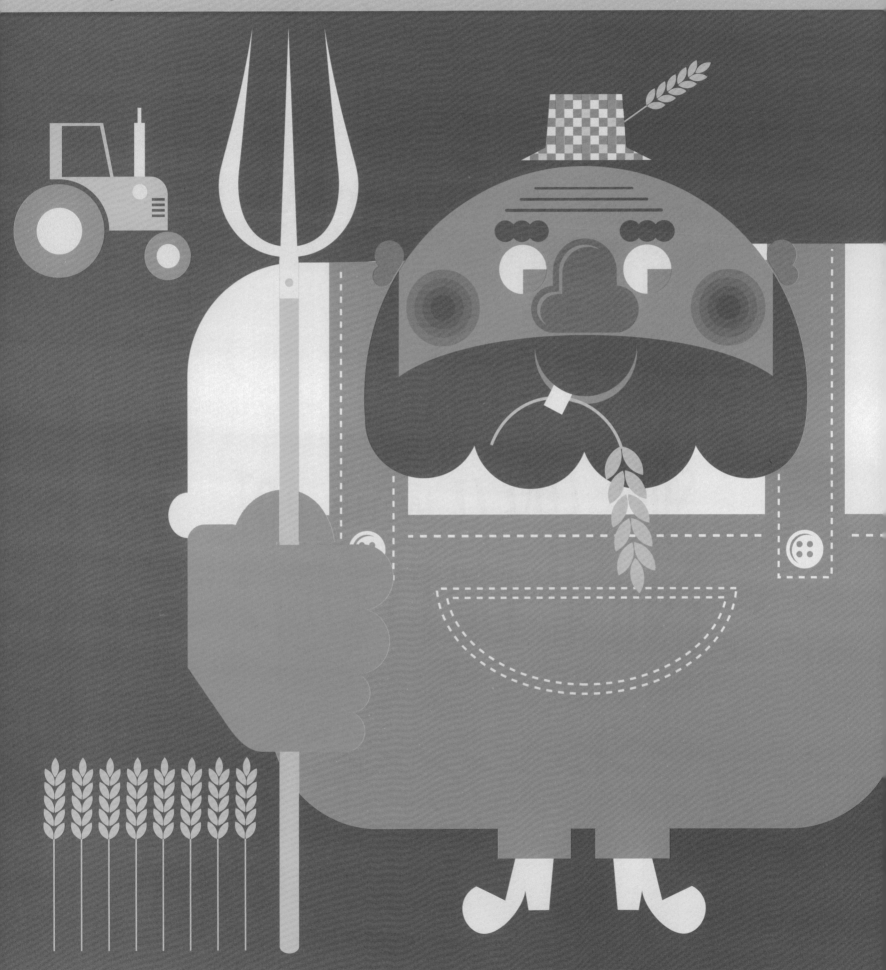

There was a farmer had a dog,
And Bingo was his name-o.
B-I-N-G-O!
B-I-N-G-O!
B-I-N-G-O!
And Bingo was his name-o!

There was a farmer had a dog...
(clap)-I-N-G-O! (x 3)
And Bingo was his name-o!

There was a farmer had a dog...
(clap)-(clap)-N-G-O! (x 3)
And Bingo was his name-o!

There was a farmer had a dog...
(clap)-(clap)-(clap)-G-O! (x 3)
And Bingo was his name-o!

There was a farmer had a dog...
(clap)-(clap)-(clap)-(clap)-O! (x 3)
And Bingo was his name-o!

There was a farmer had a dog...
(clap)-(clap)-(clap)-(clap)-(clap)! (x 3)
And Bingo was his name-o!

A sailor went to sea, sea, sea,
To see what he could see, see, see;
But all that he could see, see, see,
Was the bottom of the deep blue sea, sea, sea!

A sailor went to chop, chop, chop,
To see what he could chop, chop, chop;
But all that he could chop, chop, chop,
Was the bottom of the deep blue chop, chop, chop!

A sailor went to knee, knee, knee,
To see what he could knee, knee, knee;
But all that he could knee, knee, knee,
Was the bottom of the deep blue knee, knee, knee!

A sailor went to sea, chop, knee,
To see what he could see, chop, knee;
But all that he could see, chop, knee,
Was the bottom of the deep blue sea, chop, knee!

CHORUS:
HERE WE GO LOOBY LOO,
HERE WE GO LOOBY LIGHT;
HERE we go looby loo,
ALL ON A SATURDAY NIGHT.

YOU PUT YOUR RIGHT ARM IN,
YOU PUT YOUR RIGHT ARM OUT;
YOU SHAKE IT A LITTLE, A LITTLE,
And turn yourself about.
CHORUS

YOU PUT YOUR LEFT ARM IN...

CHORUS

YOU PUT YOUR RIGHT LEG IN...

Chorus

YOU PUT YOUR LEFT LEG IN...

Chorus

YOU PUT YOUR WHOLE SELF IN...

CHORUS

Chorus:
Lou, Lou, skip to my Lou,
Lou, Lou, skip to my Lou,
Lou, Lou, skip to my Lou,
Skip to my Lou, my darling.

Fly's in the buttermilk, shoo fly shoo,
Fly's in the buttermilk, shoo fly shoo,
Fly's in the buttermilk, shoo fly shoo,
Skip to my Lou, my darling.
Chorus

Little red wagon, painted blue, (x 3)
Skip to my Lou, my darling.
Chorus

Lost my partner, what'll I do? (x3)
Skip to my Lou, my darling.
Chorus

I'll find another one, prettier than you, (x 3)
Skip to my Lou, my darling.
Chorus

Can't get a red bird, jay bird'll do, (x 3)
Skip to my Lou, my darling.
Chorus

Cat's in the cream jar, how they chew, (x 3)
Skip to my Lou, my darling.
Chorus

Pig's in the parlour, what'll I do? (x 3)
Skip to my Lou, my darling.
Chorus

Off to Texas, two by two, (x 3)
Skip to my Lou, my darling.
Chorus

'ORANGES and LEMONS',
SAY THE BELLS OF St. Clements.
'YOU OWE ME FIVE FARTHINGS',
SAY THE BELLS OF St. Martins.

'WHEN will YOU pay ME?'
SAY THE BELLS OF Old Bailey.
'WHEN I grow RICH',
SAY THE BELLS OF Shoreditch.

'WHEN will THAT be?'
SAY THE BELLS OF Stepney.

'I do NOT KNOW,'
SAYS THE GREAT BELL OF Bow.

HERE COMES a CANDLE to LIGHT YOU TO BED,
AND HERE COMES a CHOPPER to CHOP OFF your HEAD!

CHOP CHOP CHOP CHOP
THE LAST MAN'S DEAD!

Here We Go Round the Mulberry Bush (pages 100–101)

Children dance in a circle for first verse. They act out washing clothes during the second verse. Then they repeat the first verse and dance in a cicle. They can also take it in turns to make up extra verses and act out the actions for each new verse.

London Bridge (pages 102–103)

Two children make an arch with their arms. The others pass through the arch in single file. When they reach the end they circle back around, so that they all continue to keep passing through 'the arch.' The 'arch' is then lowered at the end of each verse or at the song's end to 'catch' a player. The last player left is the winner.

A-Tisket, A-Tasket (pages 104–105)

Children dance in a circle. One child runs around the outside of the circle and drops a 'letter' on the first 'I dropped it'. Whomever it is dropped next to then picks it up and chases the child who dropped it. The child who gets to the empty place first sits down and the other child is then the one whom runs around the outside of the circle when the rhyme is sung the next time.

Pop Goes the Weasel (pages 106–109)

Children form several circles holding hands. As they sing the verse they dance around the circle. Meanwhile, single players called 'weasels' stand in the middle of each ring, with one extra player roaming around the circles (so that there is one more weasel than there are rings). When the children sing the line, 'pop goes the weasel,' they release their hands and the weasels run to stand inside a new circle. The weasel that doesn't make it into a circle is out, and the remaining players form one fewer ring and repeat this game, until there is only one weasel left, as the winner.

The Farmer in the Dell (pages 110–113)

The players form a circle holding hands and singing the first verse while moving around a single player who has been designated as 'the farmer.' When the verse is over they stop and the farmer makes his choice of a wife (sometimes without looking, by spinning around the circle with their eyes shut and pointing at someone). The wife joins him in the centre for her verse. This continues through the verses until either the cheese or dog is selected or only one person is left, to become the last character added to the centre. This person should become the farmer for the next round.

Ring-a-ring o' Roses (page 114)

Children hold hands and walk in a circle for the first three lines of the song. They all fall to the floor on 'We all fall down.'

Pease Porridge Hot (page 115)

Children divide into pairs and do the following hand-clapping sequence	
Pease	(clap both hands to thighs)
porridge	(clap own hands together)
hot	(clap partner's hands)
Pease	(clap both hands to thighs)
porridge	(clap own hands together)
cold	(clap partner's hands)
Pease	(clap thighs)
porridge	(clap own hands)
in the	(clap right hands only)
pot	(clap own hands)
Nine	(clap left hands only)
days	(clap own hands)
old	(clap partner's hands)

Bingo (pages 116–117)

In each verse the word B-I-N-G-O is spelled out, one letter is replaced with a clap, until all letters of the word are clapped.

A Sailor Went to Sea, Sea, Sea (pages 118–119)

A sailor went to sea, sea, sea...	shield your eyes one hand on each mention of the words 'sea' and 'see'
A sailor went to chop, chop, chop...	make a chopping motion of one hand against your other arm on each mention of the word 'chop'
A sailor went to knee, knee, knee...	tap your knee on each mention of the word 'knee'
A sailor went to sea, chop, knee...	make each of the appropriate motions above on each mention of the words 'sea,' 'see,' 'chop' and 'knee'

Here We Go Looby Loo (pages 120–121)

Children dance in a circle for the 'looby loo' chorus. They stop for each verse and act out the instructions: putting their right arm in and out of the circle and shaking it, then turning around before singing the chorus and dancing in a circle again. This is repeated with their left arm, each leg, and finally their whole self, as they jump in and out of the circle.

Skip to My Lou (pages 122–125)

Partners hold hands and skip around in a circle with all the other partners, with a single person in the middle of the circle. The single players sings the 'Lost my partner, what'll I do?' verse. Then the other players reply 'I'll find another one, prettier than you' and the single person grabs a partner from the closest couple. The new single person takes their place in the middle and the game repeats.

Oranges and Lemons (pages 126–127)

Two children make an arch with their arms. The other children form pairs and pass through the arch two by two, circling around once they get through the arch, to keep passing underneath. The arch is then lowered at the end the song on 'dead!' to 'catch' a pair. The caught pair stands next to the last pair and makes an arch. As the rhyme continues, each caught pair joins the arch, so it becomes longer and longer. The final pair that is not caught in the arch is the winner.

THERE WERE 10 in the BED

and OTHER COUNTING Nursery RHYMES

There were ten in the bed
And the little one said,
'Roll over! Roll over!'
So they all rolled over
And one fell out,
And he gave a little scream,
And he gave a little shout, 'Yahoo!'
Please remember to tie a knot in your pyjamas,
Single beds are only made for
One, two, three, four, five, six, seven, eight –

There were nine in the bed...
One, two, three, four, five, six, seven –

There were eight in the bed...
One, two, three, four, five, six –

There were seven in the bed...
One, two, three, four, five –

There were six in the bed...
One, two, three, four –

There were five in the bed...
One, two, three –

There were four in the bed...
One, two –

There were three in the bed...
One –

There were two in the bed
And the little one said,
'Roll over! Roll over!'
So they all rolled over
And one fell out,
And he gave a little scream,
And he gave a little shout, 'Yahoo!'
Please remember to tie a knot in your pyjamas,
Single beds are only made for one.
Single beds are only made for one.

10 GREEN BOTTLES HANGING ON THE WALL, TEN GREEN BOTTLES HANGING ON THE WALL, AND IF ONE GREEN BOTTLE SHOULD ACCIDENTALLY FALL, THERE'LL BE NINE GREEN BOTTLES HANGING ON THE WALL.

9 GREEN BOTTLES HANGING ON THE WALL, NINE GREEN BOTTLES HANGING ON THE WALL, AND IF ONE GREEN BOTTLE SHOULD ACCIDENTALLY FALL, THERE'LL BE EIGHT GREEN BOTTLES HANGING ON THE WALL.

8 GREEN BOTTLES HANGING ON THE WALL, EIGHT GREEN BOTTLES HANGING ON THE WALL, AND IF ONE GREEN BOTTLE SHOULD ACCIDENTALLY FALL, THERE'LL BE SEVEN GREEN BOTTLES HANGING ON THE WALL.

7 GREEN BOTTLES HANGING ON THE WALL, SEVEN GREEN BOTTLES HANGING ON THE WALL, AND IF ONE GREEN BOTTLE SHOULD ACCIDENTALLY FALL, THERE'LL BE SIX GREEN BOTTLES HANGING ON THE WALL.

6 GREEN BOTTLES HANGING ON THE WALL, SIX GREEN BOTTLES HANGING ON THE WALL, AND IF ONE GREEN BOTTLE SHOULD ACCIDENTALLY FALL, THERE'LL BE FIVE GREEN BOTTLES HANGING ON THE WALL.

5 GREEN BOTTLES HANGING ON THE WALL, FIVE GREEN BOTTLES HANGING ON THE WALL, AND IF ONE GREEN BOTTLE SHOULD ACCIDENTALLY FALL, THERE'LL BE FOUR GREEN BOTTLES HANGING ON THE WALL.

4 GREEN BOTTLES HANGING ON THE WALL, FOUR GREEN BOTTLES HANGING ON THE WALL, AND IF ONE GREEN BOTTLE SHOULD ACCIDENTALLY FALL, THERE'LL BE THREE GREEN BOTTLES HANGING ON THE WALL.

3 GREEN BOTTLES HANGING ON THE WALL, THREE GREEN BOTTLES HANGING ON THE WALL, AND IF ONE GREEN BOTTLE SHOULD ACCIDENTALLY FALL, THERE'LL BE TWO GREEN BOTTLES HANGING ON THE WALL.

2 GREEN BOTTLES HANGING ON THE WALL, TWO GREEN BOTTLES HANGING ON THE WALL, AND IF ONE GREEN BOTTLE SHOULD ACCIDENTALLY FALL, THERE'LL BE ONE GREEN BOTTLE HANGING ON THE WALL.

1 GREEN BOTTLE HANGING ON THE WALL, ONE GREEN BOTTLE HANGING ON THE WALL, AND IF ONE GREEN BOTTLE SHOULD ACCIDENTALLY FALL, THERE'LL BE NO GREEN BOTTLES HANGING ON THE WALL.

Chook, chook, chook-chook-chook,

Good morning Mrs Hen,

How many chickens have you got?

Madam, I've got ten.

Four of them are yellow,

And four of them are brown,

And two of them are speckled red,

The nicest in the town.

Five little monkeys,
Jumping on the bed;
One fell off
And bumped his head.
Mama called the doctor,
The doctor said:
'No more monkeys
Jumping on the bed!'

Four little monkeys,
Jumping on the bed…

Three little monkeys,
Jumping on the bed…

Two little monkeys,
Jumping on the bed…

One little monkey,
Jumping on the bed…

One, two, three, four, five,
Once I caught a fish alive;
Six, seven, eight, nine, ten,
Then I let it go again.

Why did you let it go?
Because it bit my finger so.
Which finger did it bite?
This little finger on the right.

THIS OLD MAN, HE PLAYED **1**

HE PLAYED KNICK-KNACK ON MY THUMB

CHORUS: WITH A KNICK-KNACK *paddywhack* GIVE THE DOG A BONE THIS OLD MAN CAME ROLLING HOME

this OLD MAN, HE PLAYED **2** HE PLAYED *knick-knack* ON MY **SHOE** CHORUS

THIS OLD MAN, HE PLAYED **3** *he played* **KNICK-KNACK** *on my knee* CHORUS

THIS OLD MAN, HE PLAYED **4** HE PLAYED KNICK~KNACK *on my* DOOR CHORUS

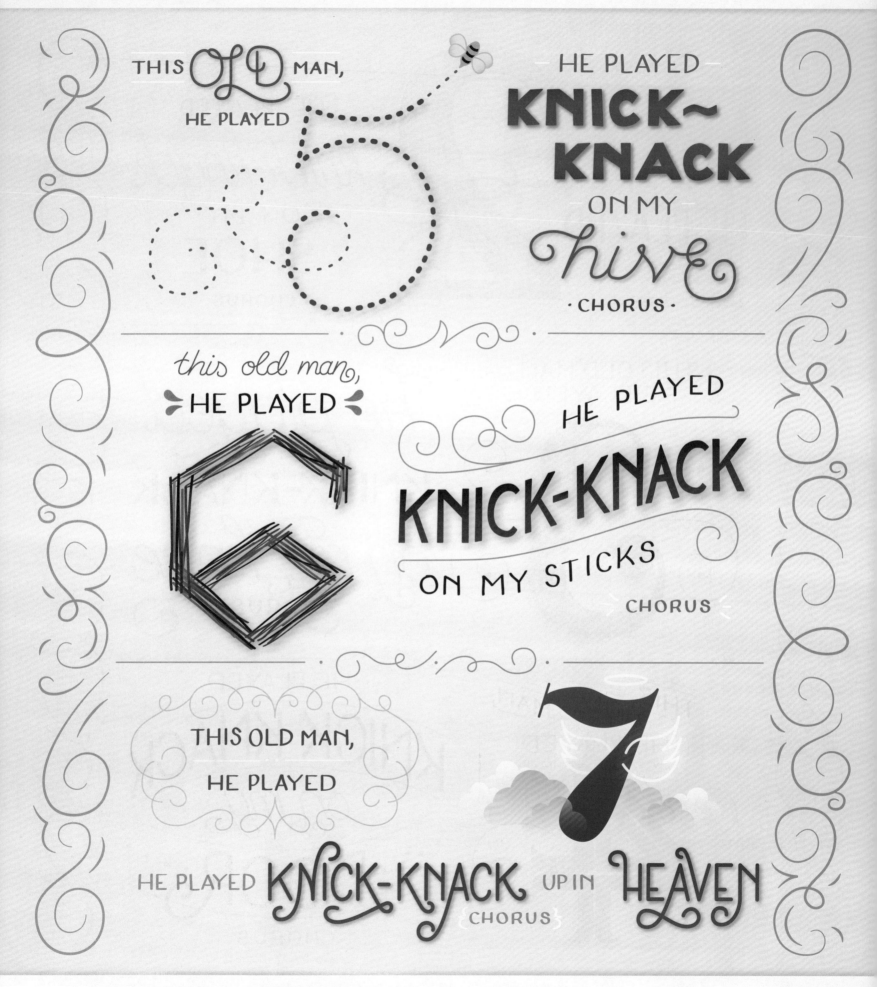

THIS OLD MAN, HE PLAYED 5 HE PLAYED KNICK~KNACK ON MY hive · CHORUS ·

this old man, HE PLAYED 6 HE PLAYED KNICK-KNACK ON MY STICKS CHORUS

THIS OLD MAN, HE PLAYED 7 HE PLAYED KNICK-KNACK UP IN HEAVEN CHORUS

THIS OLD MAN, HE PLAYED
8

HE PLAYED
knick-knack
ON MY GATE
CHORUS

this
OLD MAN,
he played
9

HE PLAYED
KNICK-KNACK
ON MY SPINE
CHORUS

THIS OLD MAN,
HE PLAYED
10

he played
KNICK-KNACK
once again
CHORUS

One elephant went out to play,
Upon a spider's web one day.
He had such enormous fun,
That he called for another elephant to come.

Two elephants went out to play,
Upon a spider's web one day.
They had such enormous fun,
That they called for another elephant to come.

Three elephants went out to play...

Four elephants went out to play...

Five elephants went out to play,
Upon a spider's web one day.
The web went creak, the web went crack,
And five elephants came running back!

Five little ducks went out one day
Over the hills and far away.
Mother duck said, 'Quack quack, quack quack!'
But only four little ducks came back.

Four little ducks went out one day
Over the hills and far away.
Mother duck said, 'Quack quack, quack quack!'
But only three little ducks came back.

Three little ducks went out one day
Over the hills and far away.
Mother duck said, 'Quack quack, quack quack!'
But only two little ducks came back.

Two little ducks went out one day
Over the hills and far away.
Mother duck said, 'Quack quack, quack quack!'
But only one little duck came back.

One little duck went out one day
Over the hills and far away.
Mother duck said, 'Quack quack, quack quack!'
But none of those five little ducks came back.

Mother duck she went out one day
Over the hills and far away.
Mother duck said, 'Quack quack, quack quack!'
And all of those five little ducks came back.

ONE, TWO, BUCKLE MY SHOE;
THREE, FOUR, knock on the door;

FIVE, SIX, PICK UP STICKS;
SEVEN, EIGHT, LAY THEM STRAIGHT;
NINE, TEN,
A GOOD FAT HEN.

ELEVEN, TWELVE,
DIG AND DELVE;
THIRTEEN, FOURTEEN,
MAIDS A-COURTING;
FIFTEEN, SIXTEEN,
MAIDS IN THE KITCHEN;
SEVENTEEN, EIGHTEEN,
MAIDS A-WAITING;
NINETEEN, TWENTY,
MY PLATE'S empty.

Three blind mice, three blind mice
See how they run! See how they run!
They all ran after the farmer's wife,
Who cut off their tails with a carving knife;
Did you ever see such a thing in your life,
As three blind mice?

The ants go marching one by one, hurrah, hurrah,
The ants go marching one by one, hurrah, hurrah,
The ants go marching one by one,
The little one stops to suck his thumb

Chorus:
And they all go marching down to the ground
To get out of the rain, BOOM! BOOM! BOOM!

The ants go marching two by two, hurrah, hurrah...
The little one stops to tie his shoe
Chorus

The ants go marching three by three, hurrah, hurrah...
The little one stops to climb a tree
Chorus

The ants go marching four by four, hurrah, hurrah...
The little one stops to shut the door
Chorus

The ants go marching five by five, hurrah, hurrah...
The little one stops to take a dive
Chorus

The ants go marching six by six, hurrah, hurrah...
The little one stops to pick up sticks
Chorus

The ants go marching seven by seven, hurrah, hurrah...
The little one stops to pray to heaven
Chorus

The ants go marching eight by eight, hurrah, hurrah...
The little one stops to shut the gate
Chorus

The ants go marching nine by nine, hurrah, hurrah...
The little one stops to check the time
Chorus

The ants go marching ten by ten, hurrah, hurrah...
The little one stops to say 'The End'
Chorus

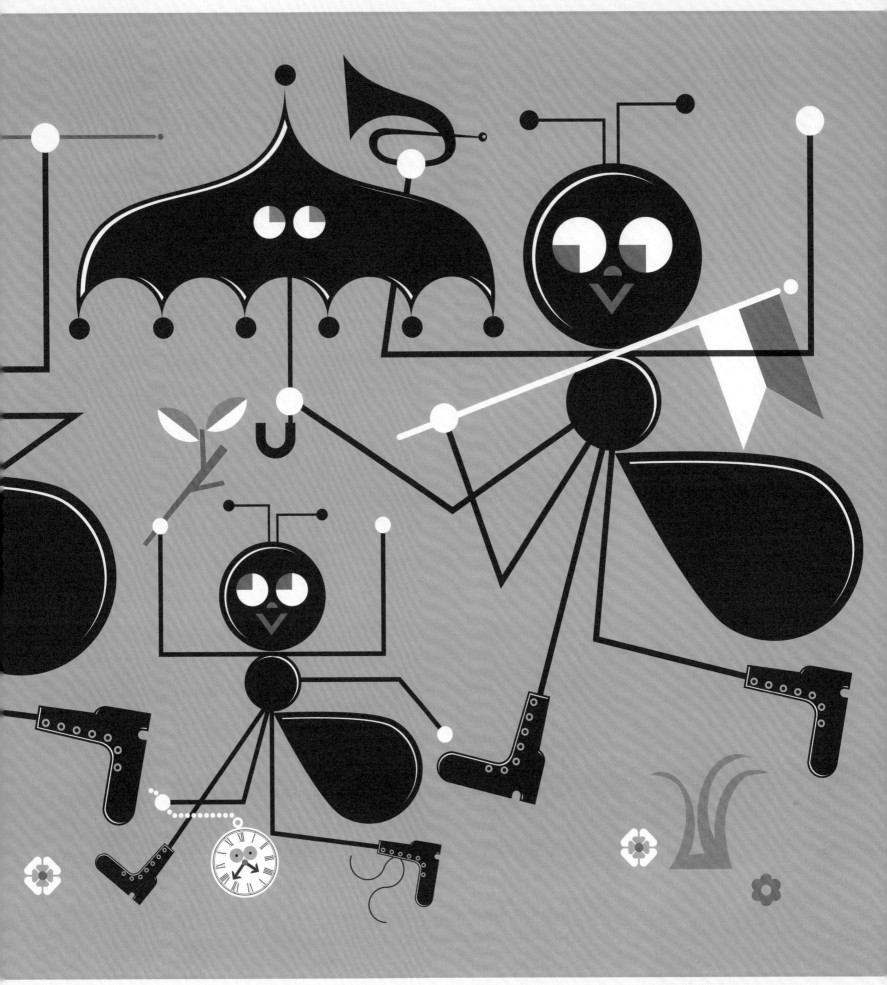

5 Five currant buns in a baker's shop,
Round and **fat** with a cherry on top,
Along came a boy with a penny one day,
Bought a currant bun and took it away.

4 Four currant buns in a baker's shop,
Round and **fat** with a cherry on top,
Along came a girl with a penny one day,
Bought a currant bun and took it away.

3 Three currant buns in a baker's shop,
Round and **fat** with a cherry on top,
Along came a boy with a penny one day,
Bought a currant bun and took it away.

2 Two currant buns in a baker's shop,
Round and **fat** with a cherry on top,
Along came a girl with a penny one day,
Bought a currant bun and took it away.

1 One currant bun in a baker's shop,
Round and **fat** with a cherry on top,
Along came a boy with a penny one day,
Bought a currant bun and **took it away.**

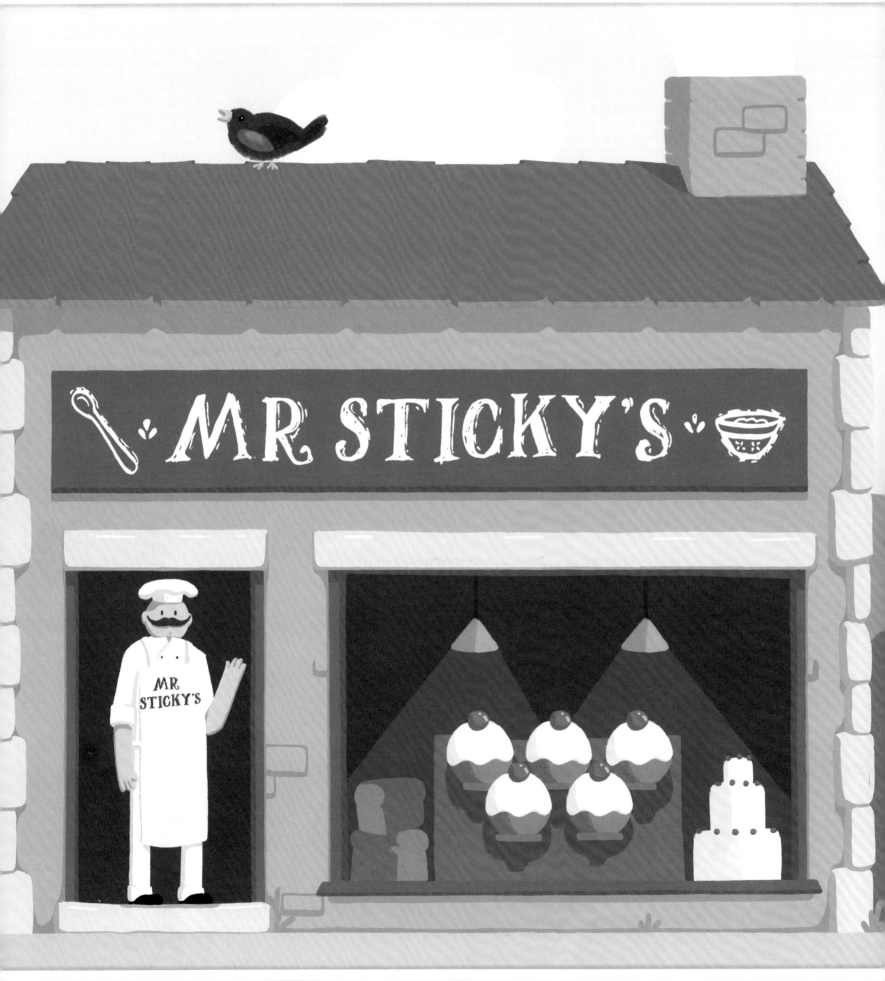

One man went to mow,
Went to mow a meadow;
One man and his dog, Spot,
Went to mow a meadow.

Two men went to mow,
Went to mow a meadow;
Two men, one man and his dog, Spot,
Went to mow a meadow.

Three men went to mow...

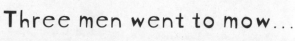

Four men went to mow...

Five men went to mow...

Six men went to mow...

Seven men went to mow...

Eight men went to mow...

Nine men went to mow...

Ten men went to mow...

One for sorrow
Two for joy
Three for a girl
Four for a boy
Five for silver
Six for gold
Seven for a secret
Never to be told

Twinkle, Twinkle, Little Star

and Other Nursery Rhyme Lullabies

Twinkle twinkle little star
How I wonder what you are
Up above the world so high

Like a diamond in the sky
Twinkle twinkle little star
How I wonder what you are

Hush-a-bye, don't you cry,
Go to sleep, little baby.
When you wake
You shall have
All the pretty little horses,
Black and bays, dapples and greys,
Coach and six white horses.

Hush-a-bye, don't you cry,
Go to sleep, little baby.
When you wake
You shall have cake
And all the pretty little horses.

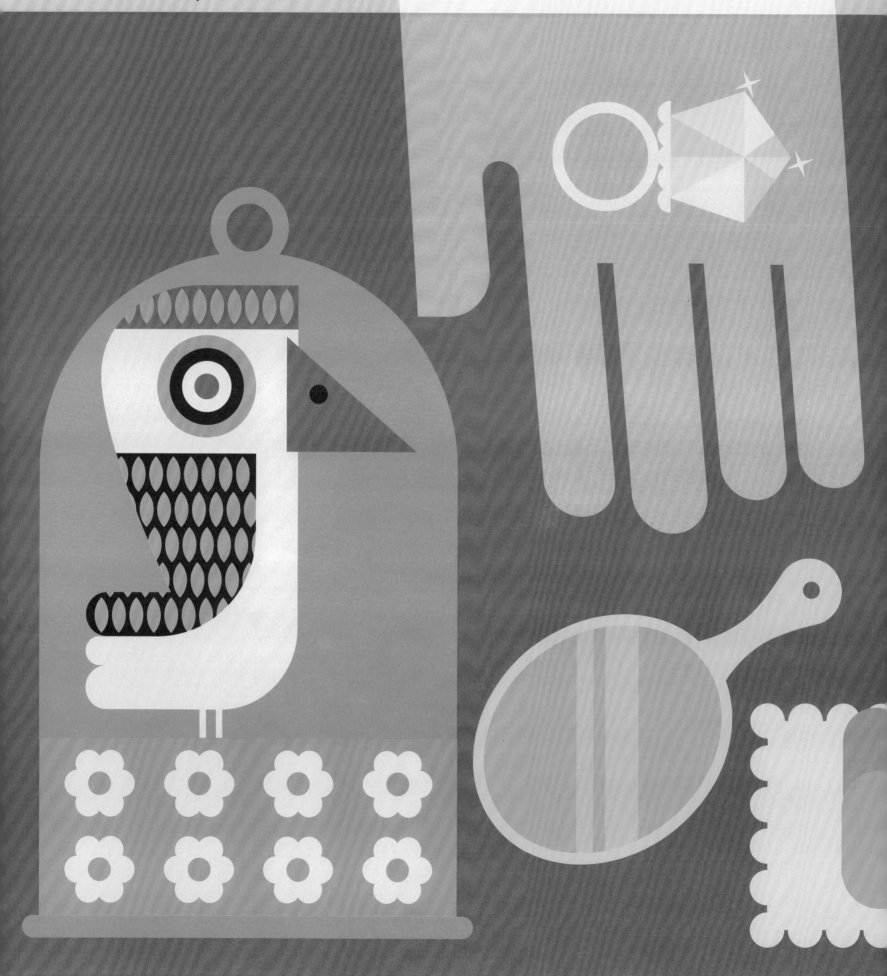

Hush, little baby, don't say a word,
Papa's going to buy you a mockingbird.

If that mockingbird won't sing,
Papa's going to buy you a diamond ring.

If that diamond ring turns brass,
Papa's going to buy you a looking glass.

If that looking glass gets broke,
Papa's going to buy you a billy goat.

If that billy goat won't pull,
Papa's going to buy you a cart and bull.

If that cart and bull turn over,
Papa's going to buy you a dog named Rover.

If that dog named Rover won't bark,
Papa's going to buy you a horse and cart.

If that horse and cart fall down,
You'll still be the sweetest little baby in town.

Day is done, gone the sun
From the lakes, from the hills, from the sky;
All is well, safely rest,
God is nigh.

Fading light dims the sight
And a star gems the sky, gleaming bright.
From afar, drawing near,
Falls the night.

Thanks and praise for our days,
'Neath the sun, 'neath the stars, 'neath the sky
As we go, this we know,
God is nigh.

Then good night, peaceful night,
Till the light of the dawn shineth bright;
God is near, do not fear,
Friend, good night.

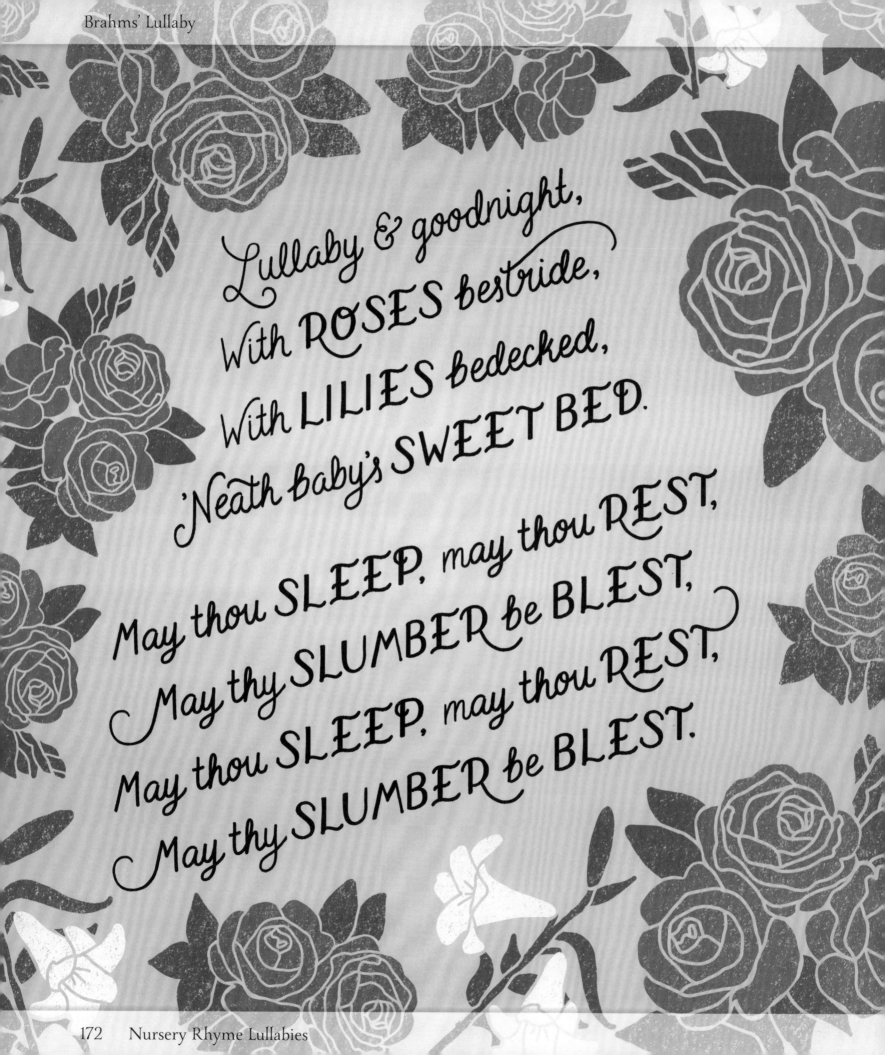

Lullaby & goodnight,
With ROSES bestride,
With LILIES bedecked,
'Neath baby's SWEET BED.

May thou SLEEP, may thou REST,
May thy SLUMBER be BLEST,
May thou SLEEP, may thou REST,
May thy SLUMBER be BLEST.

Lullaby & goodnight,
Thy MOTHER'S delight.
Bright ANGELS around
My DARLING shall GUARD.

They will GUIDE thee from HARM,
Thou art SAFE in my ARMS.
They will GUIDE thee from HARM,
Thou art SAFE in my ARMS.

Frère Jacques,
  Frère Jacques,
Dormez-vous?
  Dormez-vous?
Sonnez les matines!
  Sonnez les matines!
Ding, dang, dong!
  Ding, dang, dong!

Are you sleeping,
  Are you sleeping,
Brother John?
  Brother John?
Morning bells are ringing!
  Morning bells are ringing!
Ding, dang, dong!
  Ding, dang, dong!

Sleep my child and peace attend thee,
all through the night.
Guardian angels God will send thee,
all through the night.

Soft the drowsy hours are creeping,
hill and vale in slumber steeping,
I my loving vigil keeping,
all through the night.

WHILE THE moon HER WATCH IS KEEPING,
ALL THROUGH THE night
WHILE THE weary WORLD IS SLEEPING,
ALL THROUGH THE NIGHT.
O'ER THE SPIRIT gently STEALING,
Visions OF DELIGHT REVEALING,
BREATHES A PURE AND HOLY feeling
ALL THROUGH THE night

Little Boy Blue,
Come blow your horn,
The sheep's in the meadow,
The cow's in the corn.

Where is the boy
Who looks after the sheep?
He's under the haystack,
Fast asleep.

Will you wake him?
No, not I.
For if I do,
He's sure to cry.

Sleep, baby, sleep,
Thy father guards the sheep,
Thy mother shakes the dreamland tree,
And from it fall sweet dreams for thee.
Sleep, baby, sleep.

Sleep, baby, sleep,
Our cottage vale is deep.
The little lamb is on the green,
With woolly fleece so soft and clean.
Sleep, baby, sleep.

Sleep, baby, sleep,
Down where the woodbines creep.
Be always like the lamb so mild,
A kind and sweet and gentle child.
Sleep, baby, sleep.

BYE, BABY bunting,

DADDY'S GONE A-HUNTING,

GONE TO GET A RABBIT SKIN,

To wrap his BABY BUNTING IN.

Golden Slumbers kiss your eyes,
Smiles await you when you rise.
Sleep, pretty baby, do not cry,
And I will sing a lullaby.

Cares you know not, therefore sleep,
While over you a watch I'll keep.
Sleep, pretty darling, do not cry,
And I will sing a lullaby.

Rock-a-bye, baby, on the tree top,
When the wind blows, the cradle will rock;
When the bough breaks, the cradle will fall,
Down will come baby, cradle and all.

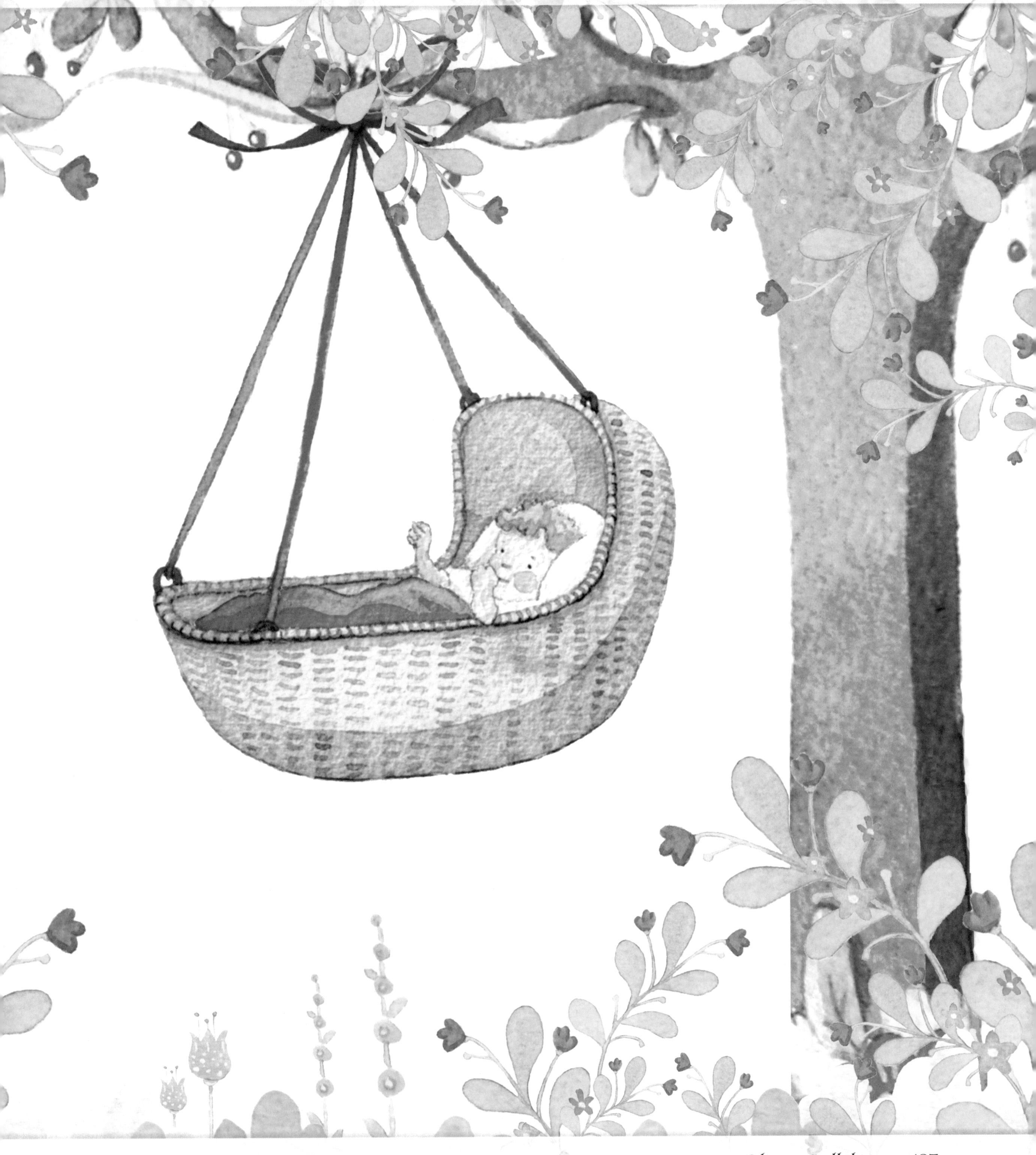

I see the MOON;
The MOON sees me.
God bless the MOON,
And God bless me.

I see the stars;
The stars see me.
God bless the stars,
And God bless me.

I see the world;
The world sees me.
God bless the world,
And God bless me.

I know an angel
Watches over me.
God bless the angels,
And God bless me.

star
light,
bright, first star I see
tonight, I wish I may,
starbright,
I wish I might,
have the wish
tonight.
I wish

The End